PLAYDATE PALS

BEAR LEARNS TO SHARE

Rosie Greening • Dawn Machell

make believe ideas

Bear was **excited** because it was his birthday.

He had invited his friends to his party.

Soon **Bear's** friends arrived
and gave him some presents.

"Happy birthday, **Bear**!" they said.

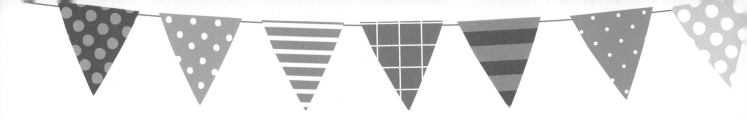

Bear started to open his presents.

His friends had got him:
a bouncy ball . . .

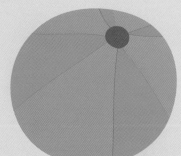

a pair of walkie-talkies . . .

and a big cake!

Bear bounced the ball on the ground.

"Can I play too?"
asked Kitten.

But **Bear wouldn't throw** her the ball!

Then **Bear** picked up the walkie-talkies.

"Can I have a turn?" asked Alligator.

But **Bear** put the walkie-talkies in his **pockets**.

Bear's friends were **sad** that they couldn't play with **Bear**.

They started to **play together** in a corner.

Soon **Bear** wanted to play catch.

But his friends were busy playing a different game, so there was **no one** to catch the ball!

Then **Bear** wanted to try the walkie-talkies.

But he had **nobody** to talk to!

He felt **sorry** that he hadn't **shared** his toys.

Bear took the toys over to his friends.
"I'm **sorry** that I didn't **share**," he said.

Bear and his friends played catch
and had fun with the walkie-talkies!

When they had finished, **Bear shared** his birthday cake with everyone.

He realized that his birthday was much more fun when he had friends to **share** it with!

READING TOGETHER

Playdate Pals have been written for parents, caregivers, and teachers to share with young children who are beginning to explore the feelings they have about themselves and the world around them.

Each story is intended as a springboard to emotional discovery and can be used to gently promote further discussion around the feeling or behavioral topic featured in the book.

Bear Learns to Share is designed to help children learn about the importance and impact of sharing. Once you have read the story together, go back and talk about any experiences the children might have in common with Bear. Talk to children about sharing and then encourage them to do so in other trusted relationships.

Look at the pictures

Talk about the characters. Do they look sad or happy when Bear doesn't share? What about when he does share?
Help children think about how sharing affects others.

Words in bold

Throughout each story there are words highlighted in bold type. These words specify either the **character's name** or useful words and phrases relating to **sharing.** You may wish to put emphasis on these words or use them as reminders for parts of the story you can return to and discuss.

Questions you can ask

To prompt further exploration of this behavioral topic, you could try asking children some of the following questions:

- If I give you some of my apple, am I sharing?
- Can you think of something you could share?
- How do you feel when your friends don't share?
- What is good about sharing?